Nobody Wants Barkley

by Marilyn D. Anderson

illustrated by Estella Lee Hickman

For my nieces—
Katie, Brenda, Meagan, and Joni

Published by Willowisp Press, Inc.
401 E. Wilson Bridge Road, Worthington, Ohio 43085

Copyright© 1990 by Willowisp Press, Inc.

Printed in the United States of America

10 9 8 7 6 5 4 3 2 1

ISBN 0-87406-459-7

One

"RUFF, ruff!" Barkley announced. He was watching the big, black-and-white creatures in the field. He wanted his master, Jamie Boggs, to do something to make the creatures go away. He looked pleadingly up at Jamie, who was busy tying his shoes. "Ruff," he tried again.

"No, Barkley," Jamie said, using one of the commands that Barkley knew. "Those are just cows, and they're supposed to be in that field."

The whiskery-faced schnauzer stopped barking. He crouched down and wiggled his way toward Jamie. He leaned against Jamie's chest and licked his face to show that he was sorry for making such a fuss. *How is a city dog supposed to know what to do when he sees monsters?* Barkley wondered.

It had been two months since Barkley's family moved all the way from beautiful Elm Street in New York to Indiana. Sometimes, it felt like it had been years since they left Elm Street, Barkley thought sadly.

Jamie and his parents had driven out to Indiana in early June, and Barkley was supposed to be flying out on an airplane to join them. But the dog had gotten out of his carrier at the airport and spent most of his time walking down dusty, hot roads and through cornfields trying to find the Boggs family.

Now that Barkley and the Boggs family were back together again, everything should have been perfect. But it wasn't at all.

Indiana was boiling hot in the summertime. And their old home was so much more fun, Barkley thought. He and Jamie used to do lots of neat things together. But in this new place, they never seemed to have any fun.

When he had first arrived, Barkley tried to liven things up. He had knocked over all the wastebaskets in the house and had gone room to room decorating with tissue paper. But no one thought it was funny. Instead, the family got mad and scolded him. Barkley didn't know what they had said, but he knew it wasn't anything nice. So, now, the dog just moped around and waited for Jamie to play with him.

That morning, Barkley had gone downstairs for breakfast as usual. He found Jamie and his mom talking in the kitchen.

"Jamie," said Mrs. Boggs, "it's such a nice day. Why don't you go outside and play?"

"By myself?" Jamie protested.

"No," she said. "Take Barkley."

Barkley's ears had perked up at the sound of his name.

"All right," Jamie said.

So, now, Barkley and Jamie were out in the yard looking for something to do. Barkley was hoping that Jamie would act like he used to and be happy.

But as soon as he finished tying his shoes, Jamie walked on ahead. Barkley trailed sadly behind him. He thought that maybe he should bark to get his master's attention, but he decided he might get into trouble again. And he hated to be yelled at!

Suddenly, Jamie stopped walking. He looked off into the woods behind the house. Barkley craned his neck to see what was so important. All the dog could see was trees.

"Did you hear some kind of animal noise, Barkley?" Jamie asked.

Barkley just looked up at him and wagged his tail cheerfully.

Then Jamie started walking faster toward the trees. Just as strangely, Jamie's steps quickened. Barkley began to trot in circles around the boy, hoping to race or play a game. But Jamie didn't seem to notice him.

They came to a barbed wire fence, and Jamie rolled underneath it. Barkley ducked his head and followed. *Oh, boy,* he thought. *We're on an adventure together at last!*

The scattered trees and blackberry thickets that dotted the hills beyond the fence were home to all kinds of animals. Barkley quickly set out to investigate each of their fascinating smells.

Jamie seemed a lot happier all of a sudden.

He started to whistle, and he picked up a stick to swing as they walked along.

After a while, Barkley spotted a small pond in the distance. He trotted toward it eagerly, thinking about taking a swim. Then, suddenly, something caught his attention. A group of woolly animals were grazing nearby. Barkley bounded joyfully toward the nearest one. The animal looked so soft and gentle.

But just as Barkley reached the fuzzy creature, it stamped its foot at him. The dog jumped back in surprise. "Ruff," he said softly.

Well, thought Barkley. *Those things look friendly, but they certainly aren't.* Barkley decided he'd better leave them alone. The animal bolted back over to where its friends were gathering in the middle of the field.

Barkley glanced back, remembering the pond. But then, he heard a loud rustling noise. He saw that all the fuzzy creatures were running in a group.

This is terrific, Barkley thought. *They want to play tag. They must have decided that I want to be their friend.* So, Barkley joined in and charged toward the group.

"Barkley! Come back here right now!" Jamie shouted loudly. But the dog didn't listen. He was having way too much fun to stop now. He couldn't understand why Jamie didn't want to join in, too.

The group of fuzzy things ran and ran. Barkley stayed close behind their heels, and Jamie tried like crazy to keep up. They ran until they came to a bunch of farm buildings.

Suddenly, a huge German shepherd appeared, and Barkley froze in his tracks. The other dog looked startled at the sight of Barkley and waited. Then a big man with dark, bushy hair and a boy about Jamie's size walked up behind the huge dog.

"What's going on here?" the man demanded. "How come this dumb mutt is chasing my flock of sheep?"

Uh-oh, Barkley thought. He knew he was in trouble again. He ran over to Jamie for help, but he sensed that his master was scared, too.

"I'm sorry, Mister," Jamie sputtered. "Barkley just wanted to play."

"Is that so?" the man asked nastily.

"I'll give you some advice, sonny," said the man, staring at Barkley. Dogs who run loose in the country and chase animals sometimes get hurt. You know what I mean?"

"Yes, sir," Jamie said quickly. "I understand. We just moved here, and I didn't know about your sheep."

"I don't want to see that dog on my property again," the man said. "Or else!"

Barkley watched as Jamie and the man talked. He wished that he could help Jamie. Then he noticed that they had stopped talking and that Jamie was looking down at him.

Jamie gave him a nod, and they both took off running back across the field. They ran until they were safely back inside their house. Jamie collapsed on the couch, and Barkley dropped to the floor nearby to pant and cool down.

Mrs. Boggs walked into the living room. "You're home already?"

"Yeah," Jamie said.

"Hmm," she said. "Well, okay. I want you to

go up and take a shower. We need to go buy you some new school clothes this afternoon."

"Can Barkley go along?" Jamie asked.

Barkley heard his name and looked up eagerly. He wagged his tail.

Jamie's mom looked down at Barkley and smiled. "Sure, I guess so."

Two

BARKLEY scrambled into the front seat beside Jamie. He was so excited to be going for a ride in the car. To say thanks, Barkley bounced around and tickled Jamie's ears with his tongue. Then he headed over to Mrs. Boggs. He wanted to be nice to her, too, so maybe she'd take him again next time.

"Barkley!" she squealed. "I have to drive. Jamie, please put him in the backseat."

"Okay, Mom," the boy agreed. He dumped Barkley onto the floor behind him. Barkley was sad. But he soon felt better. He realized that he could look out of both windows from the back. All he could see at first was a corn-field on one side and a small forest of trees on the other. But then they passed a house with some kids playing in a sandbox in the front yard. Barkley pressed his nose to the window and wagged his tail. Boy, he loved kids more than just about anything.

Next, Barkley saw a field of tall grass and another house. The house looked like it was falling apart. Some of the glass in the windows was missing. And the grass was way too high. But the old lady who rocked on the front porch swing didn't seem to mind.

"What a junky place," Jamie observed.

"Yes, I'm afraid poor old Mrs. Williams has a hard time of it," said his mother. "I've heard a lot about her."

Barkley couldn't understand what they were mumbling about, so he looked at the third house they drove by. It was a long brick house with a garage attached to the right end. Two young boys were shooting baskets in the driveway. Barkley was especially interested because the boys seemed to be having fun.

"Well, look, Jamie. There *are* some boys in this neighborhood," Mrs. Boggs pointed out. "Maybe you could meet them and play over here. Or why don't you invite them over to our house to play sometime?"

Jamie made a face and shook his head. He stared out the window and didn't say anything.

Barkley sat patiently in the car while Jamie shopped for clothes. They had left each of the windows down a little, so Barkley would stay cool. Jamie didn't look any happier when they returned to the car with four shopping bags full of stuff.

For the next couple of weeks, there were a few fun times, but all in all it had been a pretty dull summer. Barkley didn't know how much more boredom he could stand.

One morning, Barkley woke up as usual and waited for someone to give him his breakfast and some fresh water. He heard Jamie bounding toward the kitchen. Barkley put on his sweetest face and put up his paw. That sometimes worked to get attention.

But Jamie just ran by and out the back door. He yelled, "Bye, Barkley," on his way out. Barkley peeked out the door and saw Jamie climb onto the same big yellow thing that he used to on Elm Street.

Barkley got very upset, because he knew that Jamie would be gone all day. He barked and barked, but the yellow thing kept moving on down the street.

Mrs. Boggs told Barkley to be quiet and shook her finger at him. Then she went back to what she was doing. The house was so quiet that it gave Barkley the creeps.

That afternoon, when the big yellow thing returned, Barkley was sitting in the front yard waiting. Jamie ran over to him and hugged him extra hard. Barkley was thrilled. This was the way things used to be. He wagged his tail to let Jamie know he liked being hugged.

"Hi, how was school?" Jamie's mother asked as she stepped outside.

"It was gross," said the boy. He turned to Barkley. "Do you want a cookie, Barkley?" The dog heard his name and wagged his tail.

Barkley followed as Jamie led the way into the kitchen. Jamie pulled a cookie out of the cookie jar and held it over Barkley's head. Like he had been taught, Barkley raised one ear, lifted his paw, and barked just once.

Jamie grinned. "Good dog," he said, handing over the cookie. "Barkley, I'm sure glad that I have you."

* * * * *

Every day that week, Mrs. Boggs asked Jamie how school had gone when he got off the bus. And every day Jamie told her it was gross. Finally, his mom wanted to know why.

"Well, what seems to be the trouble at school?" she asked him.

Jamie shrugged his shoulders. "Well," he began slowly. "At first everybody just stared at me because I'm new. But now this kid named Devon Keeps always teases me about Barkley."

"About Barkley?" his mother asked. "How would this boy know anything about your dog?"

Jamie scuffed one foot against the other. "Oh, he lives on a farm across the woods from us," he explained. "One day, Barkley and I went over there by mistake."

"I don't really understand what there is to tease you about," said Mrs. Boggs. "The best thing to do is ignore him, and he'll probably forget about it."

* * * * *

A few days later, the Boggs family was eating supper when Jamie's mom clanked her glass and said she had an announcement to make.

The noise her spoon made when it clanked against the glass scared Barkley. He went to sit on the other side of the room.

"Guess what?" she asked. "I just found out I got the job at the real estate office. I'll be working from 9 to 3, so I'll be here when you get home from school."

"That's great, Mom," Jamie said. "But what about Barkley? You're supposed to be here to take care of him."

"Well, mothers are people, too. I loved working in Albany," she explained. "I thought I would like staying home for a while. But I like working better. Besides, Barkley can stay

17

in the garage until I get home."

Barkley's ears perked up when he heard his name. Was it good news? Was Jamie taking him out for a walk? Or was he in trouble again for something that he didn't even know about?

"He can't stay in the garage," Jamie protested. "It's really gross out there."

"He'll be just fine," Mr. Boggs spoke up. "If we try to tie him up out back, he always digs holes or gets away. I think that would be worse."

"But he'll hate the garage," Jamie whined.

"Well, son, it can't be helped this time," Mr. Boggs said. "You know what might happen if Barkley ran around loose."

"I know," answered Jamie. "That mean man said Barkley might get hurt. I think he might hurt Barkley."

Mr. Boggs nodded. "Let's try it for now," he said. "We don't want anything to happen to Barkley."

The next morning, Mrs. Boggs left even before Jamie was finished dressing for school. His father reminded him to put Barkley in the garage before he left on the school bus.

Jamie looked down at Barkley, who lay near his feet. "I'm sorry about this whole mess, Barkley," he told him. "I'd be glad to skip school and take care of you. But there's no way Mom and Dad would go for that."

Jamie slowly led the way into the garage. From the tone of his master's voice, Barkley knew that whatever was going on wasn't good news. There wouldn't be any excitement today. He could tell. But he *wasn't* prepared for the garage.

"I know it's pretty crummy in here. I brought out your rug. I hope it helps a little," Jamie said. He kneeled down to hug the dog. "You have to stay in here. If you run away, you might get in trouble. Mom and Dad might even have to get rid of you if you're bad."

Barkley could tell by Jamie's voice that the boy was a little bit scared.

"Jamie, hurry up," Mr. Boggs called from the house. "The bus is coming down the street."

"Okay," he answered. "Bye, Barkley." Jamie

closed the door behind him.

"Awwwrrr!" Barkley protested. But no matter what sounds he made, the door stayed closed. He heard the bus pull away and Mr. Boggs's car starting. He realized that they weren't coming back to get him.

Suddenly, Barkley had a terrible thought. *What if they never came back to get me?*

"AWWWRRR!" he called out again. But nobody paid any attention to him. *Nobody wants me,* Barkley thought. *Nobody cares about me. If they liked me, they wouldn't make me stay out here.*

He put his head on his paws and whimpered quietly for a long time. Finally, he was all tired out from whimpering and crying. He decided to check out the place and find out how bad it really was.

The smell of oil hit Barkley's tender nose as he looked over the oil cans that lined the floor. Fruit jars rocked about when he brushed against the wooden shelf where they sat. A rake fell and nearly hit him on the head.

Barkley leaped away and ducked beneath

an old chair. It was a big wooden thing with space under it. It looked something like the one Jamie had in his bedroom. Then he noticed there was a desk behind the chair he was hiding under.

Barkley thought the open space looked interesting, so he crawled back into it as far as he could and snuggled into a ball. Then he settled down to take a nap. After a few minutes, though, his paws started to hurt from the cold, hard floor.

He walked out and sat on his rug. He looked back and forth between his rug and the little space where he had been laying. *No, it wouldn't fit in there*, he decided.

Barkley walked back over toward the desk, then noticed some rags hanging from the wall behind him. He pulled at one until it fell at his feet. He slowly dragged it into the cubbyhole and made himself a bed. When he was satisfied, he plopped down in the middle.

Ooh, he thought. *This was more like it!* He decided that if he had to stay here, he might as well get comfortable.

Three

WHEN Jamie opened up the big garage door later that afternoon, Barkley was thrilled to see him.

They had fun together for the rest of the day.

Barkley awoke the next morning and gave his master's face a lick. He wanted to show him that he was being a good sport, even though he had been locked in the garage for a whole day.

But as soon as Jamie had finished his breakfast, he led Barkley back out to the garage again. Barkley was upset at first, because he thought he was being punished. But he remembered his nest beneath the desk and immediately curled up for a long nap.

His spot was almost perfect, but it still

needed a little more padding. He reached up and tugged at another rag that hung on the wall. This one wouldn't budge though. Barkley pulled and pulled. Finally, all at once, a whole wad of cloth came loose and Barkley slammed against the desk. "Ruff!" he growled.

He got up and shook himself off. He sniffed to make sure he hadn't landed in anything weird. It was then that he noticed the smell of fresh air. He looked around until he saw where it was coming from. There was a big hole in the garage wall where the rags had been. *Oops*, he thought, *the rags must have been stuck in that hole on purpose.*

Barkley jumped up on his hind legs and leaned against the wall. He looked through the opening. He could see the woods behind the house. The hole seemed pretty big. *Maybe I could squeeze through there*, Barkley thought.

He squeezed his eyes shut tightly to concentrate. Then, in a split second, he opened his eyes and leaped up and through the hole in the wall. He rolled over and over as he landed

on the grassy ground. He had done it! He was outside!

Barkley stood up and leaped around in the sunshine. Then he raced around and around the house barking to tell everyone how happy he was. He thought for a second that maybe someone would come out and put him back in the garage. But no one did.

It sure felt good to be outside. But Barkley wanted someone to play with him.

Hey, what about those kids I saw playing a while ago? Barkley wondered, remembering his ride in the car. Maybe they would play with him. So, off he went to find them.

Sure enough, the kids were playing in front of their house. He bounded up to them, wearing his sweetest look. The kids immediately pointed to him and gathered around to pet him. Then, one little boy ran toward him yelling, "Doggie, Doggie."

Barkley wagged his tail and rolled over on his back. Boy, was that a mistake! The little boy threw himself right on top of Barkley, and groped his sticky fingers through the dog's curly fur. He grabbed Barkley's nose and began to twist it. That hurt, and Barkley growled at him.

Then, a little girl came up to him.

"Puppy," she screeched as she sat down on Barkley, too. Her tiny fingers pulled his tail. The schnauzer was scared. He tried to kick himself free, but he was stuck.

Suddenly, Barkley heard a door slam.

"Zachary, Maria, get away from that dirty dog!" a woman's voice screeched. Barkley could see that the woman was coming toward them with a broom in her hand.

Zachary turned to look at his mother and relaxed his grip. Barkley saw his chance. He squirmed and wiggled himself away from the kids. He raced out of the yard as fast as he could and headed for home.

"Get out of here, you mutt," the woman yelled after him. "And don't ever come back!"

Barkley had had enough for one day. He galloped to the garage and crawled back inside. He fell fast asleep. But he kept seeing the angry face of that woman with the broom.

* * * * *

"Hi," Mrs. Boggs said when Jamie came home from school. "How was school today?"

"Okay, I guess," Jamie said. He quickly changed the subject. "Can I join the 4-H Club, Mom? The first meeting is tonight."

"Well, sure, honey," she said, looking pleased.

"They have a dog training project," he said "and I want to show those other kids how smart Barkley really is."

Four

RIGHT after supper, Jamie walked over to the cupboard and brought out Barkley's grooming brush. Barkley wagged his tail eagerly. He loved to feel the brush bristles scratch his back.

Jamie sat down on the couch, and Barkley sat on the floor in front of him. Jamie always started near Barkley's neck and brushed all the way through his fur. But this time Jamie ran into trouble.

He looked at Barkley's fur more closely and saw that there was a purplish mess in Barkley's fur. "Gross, what is this?" Jamie asked. "Yuck! It looks like grape jelly." Jamie said.

Barkley felt Jamie trying to tug the brush through his fur. It even hurt a little. It had never hurt before when Jamie brushed his hair.

Then Barkley remembered those kids who had jumped on him and pulled at his tail. Their hands were sticky and gooey. Maybe some of that stuff got into his fur, making it hard to brush. He decided he'd never, ever go back to that house again, not even if he was really lonely.

A little while later, Barkley found himself in the car again with Jamie and Mrs. Boggs. They drove until they stopped in front of a big building. Barkley thought it looked like the one he'd been in at the airport when he had gotten lost.

"Here we are at the fairgrounds. Do you want me to go in with you?" Mrs. Boggs asked.

"No, the other kids will think I'm a sissy," Jamie said as he got out of the car with Barkley.

"Okay, then I'll see you at about 8:30. Have fun," she said as she waved good-bye.

Jamie sighed and stared at the building. He seemed really worried about going inside.

Barkley started to get nervous, too. The dog paced and sat and paced and sat.

Finally, a shiny blue car drove up. A girl with a beautiful golden retriever got out. The girl glanced at Jamie, then at Barkley. The dogs touched noses, and Barkley wagged his tail.

"Hi," said the girl. "You're new, aren't you?"

"Yeah," said Jamie.

"What kind of a dog is that?" the girl asked him.

Jamie looked down at his dog. "He's a schnauzer. His name is Barkley."

"Cute," said the girl. "My dog is named Sadie, and I'm Melissa Taylor. What's your name again?" she asked.

"Jamie Boggs. I heard about the 4-H Club at school, but I don't know what I'm supposed to do."

Melissa grinned. "No problem," she said. "Just follow me, and I'll get you signed up."

Jamie followed her into the building and Barkley stuck close behind him. The building was really just a steel shell that was set on top of some dirt. The place was so big that

Barkley wondered what might be hiding in the corners.

Two women were working on a pile of papers at a small desk, and Melissa led Jamie toward them. She stopped in front of a tall, serious-looking woman.

"Mrs. Redding, this is Jamie Boggs," Melissa said.

"And this is Barkley," Jamie added. The woman smiled at Jamie and reached down to the dog. Barkley's tail wagged uncertainly.

"Welcome to our class, Jamie," said the other woman, who seemed a little friendlier than the first woman. "I'm Mrs. Terrell, and I have some papers here that your parents will have to sign."

"Can I bring the papers back to the meeting next week?" Jamie asked.

"Of course," said Mrs. Terrell. Jamie stuffed the papers into his pocket.

"Jamie, is that the only collar you have for Barkley?" Mrs. Redding asked.

Jamie looked down and shrugged. "Yeah, I guess so."

"You'll need to get one like this," Melissa told him. She worked her fingers under the chain that Sadie wore on her neck. "It's called a choke collar."

"Did you say choke?" Jamie asked with a gulp.

"Yes, but don't worry," said Mrs. Terrell. "We use choke collars to help give us better control when training the dogs. They are not used to hurt the dogs in any way."

"Here's how it works," Mrs. Redding explained. She took out a piece of chain with a ring at each end and dropped the chain through one of the rings. Then she slipped the loop she had formed over Barkley's head.

"Now you tighten this collar to help you control Barkley's movements," Mrs Terrell said.

Barkley wondered what he had done wrong this time. Why had this strange woman put such a heavy thing around his neck? It pulled at his fur.

Barkley looked around and saw that lots of other kids and their dogs were arriving.

Parents were gathering around to watch. There was noisy confusion as everyone tried to talk.

Barkley became anxious. He was tired of having his head stuck through a leash. He whined and refused to sit still. There was nothing he hated more than wearing a heavy collar—except maybe having two kids sit on him.

"Maybe you two would like to wait over by the bleachers until we're ready to begin," said Mrs. Terrell. "Melissa, could you fill Jamie in on what we'll be doing tonight?"

Melissa nodded and led Sadie toward the bleachers along the sides of the building. Jamie and Barkley followed. But, suddenly, Barkley saw that boy and his mean-looking German shepherd who lived across the woods from the Boggses. The big dog growled at them.

"Devon, please tell your dog to back off," Melissa said.

"Why should I?" the boy snapped. "It's that mutt of Jamie's he's after anyway."

"Call your dog off now, Devon, or I'll yell for

help," Melissa said nervously.

Finally, the boy shrugged his shoulders. "Back, Sarge," he commanded. Almost instantly, the shepherd stepped to his master's side.

"Wow! That was a close one," Melissa said as she and Jamie found a quiet spot near the bleachers. "Devon's dog could mean big trouble if you're not careful."

"I know," said Jamie. "They live right behind us. Barkley and I went exploring one day and ended up on their property. I thought his dog was going to bite us. And his dad warned us to stay away *or else*."

"Why does he have to be in this class?" Melissa asked.

"Who knows?" Jamie asked, shrugging his shoulders.

"Let's forget about him. I'm supposed to tell you what's going on around here," Melissa said. "I think what we're going to do is split up into two classes. Kids who have been here before will work with Mrs. Terrell, and the new kids will go with Mrs. Redding."

36

"You mean I'm not the only beginner?" Jamie asked hopefully.

Melissa grinned. "Nope. I was new last year. The classes are really fun. This year I'm even hoping to win a trophy at the county fair."

"What's that?" Jamie asked.

"Every fall there's a celebration at the school. They have a bunch of contests and a neat dog show."

"Wow! That sounds great," Jamie exclaimed. "If Barkley won something at a dog show, the kids at school would be really impressed."

Melissa laughed. "That's what I was counting on, too. But the show is only for experienced dog handlers, so you won't be able to enter until next year."

"Rats," Jamie mumbled. "Barkley needs to do something special now."

Barkley was busy trying to figure out a way to get the weird metal collar back over his head. He wanted to meet some of the other dogs and make some friends. But he intended to stay far away from that mean shepherd.

Suddenly, Barkley noticed a pretty white poodle a few feet away. He wanted to meet her. *Come on, Jamie,* Barkley thought, *let's get over there before the poodle walks away.*

Barkley began tugging on the chain to let Jamie know that it definitely was time to move on. He couldn't wait to make a new friend.

Five

BARKLEY squirmed away and moved closer to the poodle. He had decided that she was the most beautiful dog he had ever seen. The poodle stared back at Barkley. Barkley's tail was wagging cheerfully.

The two teachers tried and tried to get class started. But everyone kept talking and the new dogs started barking at each other. Finally, the teachers divided up the class.

All of the kids and dogs who had been to dog training class before went out into the parking lot with Mrs. Terrell. Jamie watched as Melissa and Sadie walked out the door. About a dozen kids and their dogs remained in the room with Mrs. Redding.

"All right," Mrs. Redding began. "I want you to form a circle around me with your dogs."

Everyone got into a circle. Barkley was right between the fluffy, white poodle and a big, friendly collie. The collie came right over to Barkley and slobbered on him.

"The first thing these dogs need to learn is the command *heel*," Mrs. Redding said. "That means whenever they walk beside you on the leash, they must keep their noses even with your left leg."

The collie was leaning toward Barkley again. This time Barkley showed him his teeth. *Don't slobber on me again,* he thought.

"When I say the word *forward*, you will tell your dog to *heel*," she continued. "Start with your left foot and do it just like this. Rover, *heel*." She started walking with an imaginary dog at her side.

Barkley sensed that something important was going on.

"Forward," Mrs. Redding commanded suddenly.

"Rover, heel," Jamie mumbled, starting off on his right foot.

Barkley was caught by surprise. *Who was*

Rover? he wondered. *And where was everyone going?* Barkley braced his feet and pawed at the leash.

"All right, hold it," Mrs. Redding ordered. "Some of us are having a little trouble. Let's all watch how my daughter Danielle does it."

Danielle turned out to be the girl with the poodle. She brought her dog to the front.

"Pixie, heel," she instructed, and away they went.

Barkley was very impressed, but not by the heeling. He thought Pixie was neat.

"Very good," Mrs. Redding praised her daughter. "Danielle was in this class last session, and she's agreed to help us with this class. See how she holds the leash in her right hand and uses her left to correct the dog."

The poodle did everything just perfectly. It even stopped and got back in line perfectly.

Mrs. Redding beamed. "Thank you, dear," she said. "All right, class. Let's try it again."

"Barkley, heel," said Jamie, remembering to use his left foot this time. But Barkley was busy investigating an interesting scent on the ground. He was trying to figure out what type of animal's scent it could be.

Then he felt a stronger tug on his neck.

"Barkley, come on," Jamie urged. He tried and tried to pull Barkley away, but Barkley refused to budge. Then a dachshund and Pixie, the white poodle, passed by them. Barkley didn't even look up.

But, suddenly, a loud growl captured Barkley's attention. "Grrr," said Sarge the German shepherd. Then he snapped at Barkley.

The little schnauzer leaped away quickly.

The scene caught Mrs. Redding's attention. "No!" she shouted. She clapped her hands loudly in the shepherd's face.

"Devon, you are going to have to be much firmer with your dog," she said sternly.

"Yes, ma'am," said the boy as he yanked the shepherd toward him sharply.

"All right, everyone. Let's try one more time, okay?" Mrs. Redding asked. "FORWARD."

Barkley's eyes were still glued to the shepherd. Jamie tugged on the leash, but Barkley hid behind his master to let his enemy walk by.

After a minute, Mrs. Redding walked over to Barkley and Jamie. "Let me try," she said, putting out her hand to take the leash.

She grasped it, then said, "Come on, Barkley, heel."

She gave him a series of sharp tugs, but he was too upset to respond. He just curled himself behind Jamie's leg. At last, Mrs. Redding shook her head and handed the leash back to Jamie.

"He's going to be a tough one," she said with a tired smile. "I wish you luck."

When class was finally over, the other kids rushed over to a table topped with punch and cookies. But Jamie and Barkley didn't care about eating. They just wanted to be left alone.

Melissa and Sadie walked over a few minutes later. "Hi, how did it go?" the girl asked as she munched a cookie.

Barkley wagged his tail slowly, but Jamie continued to stare at the floor. "Lousy," he said. "We'll never get it."

44

"Sure you will," Melissa said. "No one does it great on the first night. Hey, maybe I could come over sometime and help you with Barkley."

"Really?" Jamie asked eagerly. "That'd be great!"

"Sure," said Melissa. "It's no problem. Hey, let's go get you some food!"

Six

THE next morning, Barkley walked right into the garage without whining. He spread out on his bed of rags and waited until he heard the car engine whir to life. When he thought the coast was clear, he leaped eagerly through the hole in the garage wall. He landed firmly on the grass outside.

Barkley plopped on the front lawn for a few minutes to plan his day. He decided to wander back to the pond that he and Jamie had discovered the day they were chased away by that mean-looking German shepherd. Barkley was sure that he could sneak around without being noticed.

So he went under the fence. Barkley strolled along enjoying the fresh air. Then, suddenly, a rabbit crossed his path.

Barkley took off like a rocket after the rabbit. But the rabbit had seen him first and was a few leaps ahead of him.

Barkley chased the rabbit through the weeds, through the creek, and over a big hill. The rabbit was just inches ahead of Barkley when it screeched to a stop. Barkley skidded head first into a garden hose.

He jumped to his feet to see where the rabbit was hiding. But before he could find it, the garden hose slithered toward him. It took Barkley a second to realize that the hose had eyes, and a tongue, and that it was ALIVE! It wasn't a garden hose. It was a huge snake!

Just as the snake looked like it was ready to pounce on him, Barkley leaped into the air and fled. He rocketed away as fast as his furry little legs would carry him.

He ran until he could barely breathe. Finally, he stopped when he reached a fence. He lay there, trying to calm down.

After a few minutes, Barkley began to look around. The place looked really familiar.

"Scram!" called a woman's voice.

Oh, no! Barkley thought. *I've done it again!*

He was back at the house where the woman with the broom had yelled at him. And this was where those jelly-fingered kids lived, too.

"You dumb dog!" screeched the woman as she charged after him.

Barkley zoomed away into a tall field of grass and crouched down to hide. He stayed there, hoping the woman would go away and leave him alone. Why was she being so mean to him? Barkley wondered. He didn't want to hurt anything.

But the woman was determined. She motioned wildly with her broom and kept right on yelling. Barkley was smart enough to keep one jump ahead of her.

Finally, he didn't hear her footsteps or her screams anymore. He lay still for a while to be sure. Just as he stood up and was shaking himself off, he heard a rustling sound behind him. He whirled around and came face to face with a very old lady.

She carried a cane above her head like a club, and Barkley was terrified all over again.

Neither of them moved for a minute. Finally, the lady lowered her cane to her side.

"Oh," she said disgustedly, "it's just another stray dog. The way Susan was yelling, I thought there was a wolf out here. Come on," the woman called as she began to walk away. She used the cane to help her walk. "You can stay with me until the coast is clear."

When the woman realized that Barkley hadn't budged, she turned around and signaled with a wave of her hand for the schnauzer to follow her.

Slowly, she shuffled back to her front porch. Barkley followed at a distance to be sure that she wasn't going to raise her cane again.

The woman sat down on a porch swing. Barkley sat down on the sidewalk in front of her house. Then he realized it was the same house and the old woman that they had driven by the day they went shopping.

"So, what brings you this way, young fellow?" Mrs. Williams asked. She said it just as if she were talking to a little boy.

Barkley wondered what she was trying to

say. She sounded friendly enough, so he wagged his tail and perked up his ears.

The woman raised her chin to study the dog more closely. "I see," she said. "And what do you think of the President these days?"

Barkley panted a bit. Then he yawned until he squeaked.

"You're quite right," the woman said with a smile.

The morning passed quickly. Barkley liked the sound of the woman's voice. But after a while she went into the house. Barkley stood up, too, wondering if he should go home.

In a few minutes, though, the woman came back outside carrying two plates.

"It's lunch time," she said as she lowered herself carefully onto the swing. She set one plate next to her and held the other out for Barkley. "Want a sandwich?"

Barkley didn't have to understand that question. He sat down, raised one ear, lifted his right paw, and said, "Ruff!"

Mrs. Williams grinned and set the plate on the porch floor. Barkley practically swallowed the sandwich whole.

The old woman beamed. "Well, now, aren't you the smart one?" She began to nibble at her own sandwich, and Barkley licked his chops. The woman shook her head.

"No, that's all for now," she said.

The woman finished her lunch and set both plates next to her. Then she smiled.

"Could I pet you? she asked softly. Barkley looked up at her as she reached toward him. He moved his head to meet her hand. Boy, it felt great to have someone pet him.

The woman began to sniffle. A tear trickled down her face. "My boys always had dogs when they lived here. That was before they married and moved away. I hardly ever see them now. It gets awfully lonesome, you know."

Barkley moved in closer. He poked his head under her hand to encourage her to scratch his head. And she did.

The afternoon zoomed by. Suddenly, Barkley realized he had better get home, because Jamie would be there soon. And Barkley's secret would be out if he didn't make it home in time to jump back through the hole in the wall.

He stood up and took a few steps toward the road.

"Oh, are you sure you have to leave?" Mrs. Williams asked.

Barkley stopped, unsure what she wanted. Then he started walking toward home.

"Please come back soon," the woman called as he began his walk through the woods.

Seven

BARKLEY scurried home as fast as his legs would go. He made it back to his comfy bed beneath the desk in plenty of time.

When Jamie finally opened the garage door, Barkley saw that Melissa was with him. He was thrilled to have two people to play with. So, he did a happy dance to let them know he wanted to play.

"He acts a lot like Sadie," Melissa said with a chuckle. "Dogs sure have a lot of personality. They have a way of letting you know what they're thinking."

"Hi, fella, how was your day?" Jamie asked, scratching behind Barkley's ears. "Were you bored in here? Let's go get some cookies."

The three of them headed for the house.

"I hope Barkley starts catching on to the

lessons," Jamie said. "The first night was a big disaster. And I don't want to be the joke of the class."

"He'll catch on," Melissa said. "He seems smart enough to learn."

Jamie took down Barkley's leash and his new collar from the closet shelf. "So, what'll we work on first?" he asked.

"Let's go out front, and I'll show you," Melissa said. She led the way out the front door and down the steps.

"Here, Barkley. Come on, boy," Jamie called.

Barkley decided that they wanted to play chase, so he kept just out of their reach.

"Uh-oh," Melissa said. "He thinks we want to play."

"Wait here. I'll get another cookie," Jamie said as he took off for the house. He reappeared in a minute, waving a cookie in his hand. "Here, Barkley. How about one more cookie?"

Barkley pricked up his ears. He never turned down a cookie. He ran to get his treat. But as Jamie gave Barkley his cookie, Melissa grabbed the dog and quickly slipped the choke

55

collar over his head.

While Barkley tried to figure out why they had done this to him, Jamie stood in the position he had learned in class. Melissa patted Barkley on the head to encourage him.

"Okay, Barkley, heel," Jamie said.

Barkley was angry. He couldn't figure out why Jamie, his favorite person in the whole world, kept doing weird things to him. Jamie had asked if he wanted a cookie, then suddenly he felt his neck being jerked around. *What was going on?* Barkley wondered.

Barkley sat still, refusing to move. Jamie pulled sharply on the leash. Then Barkley lay down and made Jamie drag him.

"I don't understand this," Melissa said. "I mean, Sadie never acted that way. Let me try to work with Barkley."

"Wait, I've got it," said Jamie. "Let me run inside and get some more cookies. If anything will get Barkley moving, it's food!"

Sure enough, Jamie was right. As soon as food was dangled in front of him, Barkley did as he was asked. Of course, Barkley just moved

from point to point to get his treat. He really didn't understand what they were trying to teach him.

Soon Barkley sat still again. "Wow," said Melissa, tugging on the leash. "He's strong when he wants to be."

"Let me take him," Jamie said eagerly. "You can handle the cookies."

"I don't think Mrs. Redding would go for using cookies to get Barkley to move," Melissa said as they switched places. "You could try sneaking him cookies in class. But if the other dogs saw you had food, you'd have a stampede on your hands. You might even get trampled to death!"

"Okay, do you have any better ideas?"

"No," Melissa admitted.

"Okay, then we'll do it my way for now," Jamie said. He gave all the cookies to Melissa and showed her where to stand.

Melissa walked about 10 feet in front of Barkley, then stopped. She turned around and held the cookie in front of Barkley.

"Heel, Barkley. Heel," Jamie said.

58

Barkley looked ahead and saw that Melissa was holding all kinds of cookies. *It made the game even more fun,* he thought. Barkley tugged hard on the leash, and Jamie used all his strength to control him. Finally, Barkley got it right. Then he leaped up and claimed his reward.

"Yeah, we did it!" cheered Jamie.

They tried it again and again until they decided that Barkley had the hang of it.

"See, he's finally catching on," Melissa said.

"Yeah, wait till the other kids see us in class," Jamie yelled. "I'll show them next time."

"But there aren't any cookies in class," Melissa reminded him. "What are you going to do to get Barkley's attention?"

Jamie shrugged. "Hopefully, by that time we won't need them. He just has to understand what *heel* means before the next class. Can you come over again tomorrow night? We both need you."

Melissa nodded. "Sure, I'll be here. I wouldn't want to let you and Barkley down."

* * * * *

The next morning, Barkley quickly scurried through the garage wall and started his journey to the old lady's house. He loved being free to smell the fresh scent of flowers and trees.

Soon, he saw her house up ahead. He trotted the last distance and found her sitting on her porch swing and humming to herself. But she stopped singing when she spotted him.

"Oh, there you are," she said, just as if she had been expecting him. "I'm so glad that you're here. I wanted to show you my pretty flowers."

The old woman took a long time to get up off the swing and position her cane in front of her. She used the cane to support herself as she walked across the porch and down the three steps to the sidewalk. She walked through her overgrown grass and finally stopped at a small bed of flowers.

"Aren't they pretty?" the woman asked as she pointed to her garden. "I can't take care of them like I should anymore, but a few pretty blossoms come up every year."

Then the woman started walking again and pointing to things as she went along. Barkley liked the sound of her voice, and she seemed happy to have him along. So, he followed her through the garden and around the yard. Finally, she was ready to go back to her porch.

Just like the day before, she went inside the house and made tasty sandwiches for herself and Barkley. He gulped down his share.

After lunch, they each took a long nap. A loud thump finally woke up Barkley. He opened his eyes and looked around. Then he saw that the lady's cane had fallen.

"Ruff, ruff," Barkley said to let her know what had happened.

The lady slowly woke up. Barkley thought she looked upset when she found she couldn't reach her cane. He wanted to help.

"Oh, my," she mumbled as she squirmed toward the cane. "It's so hard for me to reach things that are on the floor."

Barkley marched over to the cane and

picked it up in his mouth. Then he walked over to her and waited as she got a good grasp on the cane. Then he let it go.

Mrs. Williams was delighted. "Oh, you are such a wonderful dog," she gushed. "I can't believe how smart you are. You're as smart as a person."

Barkley wagged his tail. He loved praise and attention. Besides cookies, they were the best things in the whole world. He trotted around proudly. Then he jumped off the porch and brought her a smaller stick.

"Oh, I'll bet you want me to throw this," the woman said with a grin. Barkley danced around and ran way out into the yard to be ready for her toss.

"All right, here it comes," she called out, tossing the stick as hard as she could. It landed about two feet from the porch, and Barkley quickly brought it back.

"Oh, what fun," she giggled. "Try to get this one."

She threw the stick again, and this time it went a little further. Barkley brought it back to her again. They were having a great time until Barkley started getting nervous about being home on time for his master.

"Will I see you tomorrow?" the lady called out as he trotted away. Barkley barked playfully at her.

Eight

O
N Friday afternoon, Barkley lay in his bed of rags in the garage. His belly was killing him!

Suddenly, he heard Jamie's voice outside the garage door.

Rats! Barkley thought. *What am I going to do? I can't be happy to see him with this terrible stomachache.*

The garage door went up and there stood Jamie. "Hey, Barkley, I'm home. And it's Friday! Yeah!"

But there was no Barkley.

"Barkley, I'm home," Jamie tried again.

Finally, Barkley tried to scamper out to greet his master. But it was no use. He fell on his side and whimpered.

"Barkley, what's wrong?" Jamie asked in a

panicky voice. "Are you sick?"

Barkley knew he was scaring Jamie, but his stomach was in knots. Mrs. Williams had made three sheets of raisin cookies, and she'd shared a dozen of them with Barkley. But there was no way he could let Jamie know that.

Sometimes being a dog isn't so easy, Barkley thought.

"Hey, Barkley, don't you want a cookie?" Jamie asked, holding one out to Barkley. The dog just shut his eyes and groaned.

"Boy, you must be sick," Jamie said. Just then, he saw his mother on the porch. He raced over and told her what had happened.

"I'm sure he'll be just fine, Jamie," his mom assured him. "Your father should be home in just a little while. He can take Barkley to the vet. I'm sorry, honey. I'd like to take him to the vet, but I have to finish getting ready for an important meeting tonight."

Jamie picked Barkley up and carefully carried him up to his bedroom. He put him on the middle of his bed and covered him with a light camping blanket. Jamie's bed was soft, and Barkley fell into a deep sleep.

Barkley woke with a start when he heard Mr. Boggs pulling his car up to the house. He slowly stood up on the bed and realized his stomachache was gone!

He jumped down from the bed to go let Jamie know that he was okay. As Barkley walked into the kitchen, he saw that Jamie was talking to his dad. It looked serious.

"Ruff, ruff," he said cheerfully. Then he put his head underneath Jamie's hand to let him know he'd like to be petted.

"Dad, he's okay," Jamie said, hugging Barkley. "I thought he was really, really sick. He wouldn't eat a cookie or anything."

"Well, let's keep an eye on him tonight just to be sure, okay?" Mr. Boggs suggested.

*　*　*　*　*

On Monday night, Jamie and Barkley headed for their second dog training class. Jamie hoped that Barkley would behave this time and do as he was told.

But when they got to class, Barkley tried to

follow Melissa to the group of experienced dogs and their owners. Barkley wanted Melissa to give him more cookies.

Jamie tugged and tugged on Barkley's collar to hold him still, while Melissa and Sadie went outside.

"All right, class," Mrs. Redding announced. "Tonight, I want you to get your dogs into the sitting position before you tell them to heel. And be sure that your dog sits again each time you stop walking."

Barkley was looking eagerly around the room for Melissa. When Jamie asked him to sit, Barkley ignored him.

"Come on, Barkley, I said SIT," Jamie said in a louder voice. He pushed hard against his dog's back end.

Barkley thought Jamie wanted to play, so he started prancing around and he jumped up on his hind legs. Jamie pushed him back down to the floor.

"Sit, Barkley," Jamie ordered as he wrestled with the schnauzer. Barkley was having a great time. He loved a wrestling match. He fought back with all four legs and licked Jamie's face when he could reach him.

Suddenly, Jamie looked up into Mrs. Redding's face. "Here, let me help you," she offered. Jamie gave her the leash.

"Barkley, sit," she commanded firmly.

From the sound of her voice, Barkley knew this woman didn't want to play. She wasn't going to be much fun. Maybe he'd better listen to her—or run to Jamie for help.

Barkley decided on the second choice. He began to tug his leash in Jamie's direction, but Mrs. Redding quickly yanked him to the ground. He whimpered as the instructor pushed him into a sitting position. Jamie's eyes grew big as he watched them.

"Don't worry, Jamie," Mrs. Redding said when she saw the fear in his eyes. "I didn't really hurt him. Whenever Barkley tries to jump up on you, all you have to do is get him in the chest with your knee. And when he won't sit, use the point of your thumb on his behind. Easy enough?"

"Uh, yeah, sure," Jamie mumbled. "It seems

easy when *you* do it."

Mrs. Redding stood up and returned to her spot at the head of the group. "Okay, everyone, FORWARD!" she called out.

Barkley looked at her and growled softly. Jamie jerked on the leash. "Barkley, HEEL!" he said loudly. This time, Jamie spoke with force and Barkley listened.

"That's much better, Jamie," Mrs. Redding said with a smile. "Okay, everbody, HALT."

Jamie stopped walking, but Barkley kept smelling around in search of his reward. *Don't I get a cookie for this?* he wondered.

"Sit," Jamie said firmly. When Barkley didn't listen, he placed his thumb near Barkley's tail and pushed. Barkley sat.

"Good dog!" Jamie said excitedly, leaning down to give Barkley a pat on the head. Barkley was thrilled to be praised and leaped around with joy.

"Oh, no," Jamie moaned. "Barkley, don't embarrass me. Listen to what I tell you, okay?"

Barkley saw the sad look on Jamie's face. He wanted to make Jamie happy. So, next time he was told to heel, he listened. And Barkley was rewarded with a scratch behind the ears and a grin from Jamie.

Mrs. Redding clapped her hands together. "Okay, gang, let's spread out into a big circle. We're going to learn some new things tonight."

All of the dogs began sniffing the air and each other. Barkley found a spot he really liked. He refused to budge a step farther.

"Barkley, heel," Jamie said. But Barkley's thoughts were elsewhere. He had spotted a collie who looked friendly and playful.

But, just then, the collie decided to play rough. He pounced right on top of Barkley. Barkley's eyes opened wide in terror as he saw the huge, hairy dog come flying toward him. He ducked out of the collie's way just in time.

Barkley tried to run. He wanted to run away fast! But his leash was stuck. It was caught firmly beneath the collie. Jamie gave the leash a tug, and the collie's owner tried to pull his dog away. Nothing worked. Soon, all four were tangled into a crazy, mangled mess.

"Hobo, please get up," pleaded the collie's

master as she tried to separate the dogs.

"Barkley," Jamie wailed.

Suddenly, Mrs. Redding left the rest of the class and came over to their group. The other kids and their dogs gathered around to delight in the mess.

"Look, it's that dumb dog of Jamie's again," a boy called out. "That stupid dog can't do anything right."

Mrs. Redding ignored the boy. She reached over to Barkley and unhooked the leash from his collar. She picked up Barkley and handed him to Jamie. Then she grabbed the collie's leash and helped it to its feet.

"Okay, there now," she said. "Please watch your dogs more carefully. Don't let them get too close to each other, or we'll be spending all of class time straightening out messes like this one. Now let's get back to work."

Class passed quickly and Barkley didn't get yelled at again. He was thrilled to see Melissa afterward, but there weren't any cookies being passed his way. *Oh well, maybe next time*, Barkley decided.

Nine

Jamie was determined to do well at the third dog training class. He and Barkley had practiced the commands together at home, sometimes with Melissa and Sadie and sometimes just the two of them.

As class got under way that evening, Mrs. Redding asked the kids to gather in the same circle they had been in the week before.

"Uh-oh," Jamie said to himself. "This is where Barkley and I got into trouble last time."

After a lot of chatter, the class was ready. Jamie looked to the left and saw a girl holding onto a sweet-looking cocker spaniel. To his right were Devon and Sarge.

"Okay, class, tonight we're going to teach your dogs to stay when they are instructed to do so," Mrs. Redding explained. "When I tell you to walk away from your dogs, be sure that they are sitting flat on the floor. You'll wave your hand in front of your dog's face and say STAY."

While Mrs. Redding talked on and on, waving her hands in the air, the German shepherd slowly moved toward Barkley. Barkley couldn't figure out why no one else saw what was happening to him.

To protect himself, Barkley scampered around Jamie's leg to the other side, where a cocker spaniel sat quietly beside its master. But Sarge inched closer and closer.

Suddenly, Devon looked down. "No," he said as he yanked Sarge back into position. "Forget about that mutt and behave."

Jamie peeled Barkley from his left leg and placed him back in the *heel* position. Barkley stood still, hoping that the mean dog would leave him alone now. *Boy, that was a close one,* he thought.

Mrs. Redding spoke again. "Okay, everyone, now walk toward the center of the circle until you come to the end of your leashes," she said. "Then turn around to face your dog, and wait. When I tell you to, go back and praise your dog. Do you all have that?"

Everyone nodded.

"Fine," she said. "Then let's make the circle bigger and try it."

Soon there was a loud and off-key chorus of "stays" ringing throughout the room. Barkley saw a hand pass in front of his eyes. Then he watched as Jamie walked away. The German shepherd looked like it wanted to move in and attack at any moment. Barkley knew that he couldn't sit there by himself. He'd be eaten or killed in seconds.

Barkley took off running after his master. When Jamie turned around and saw Barkley standing right behind him, he groaned.

"No, Barkley," Jamie said. Barkley could tell that he'd done something wrong again. But he had no idea what it could be. "This time you're going to stay, do you understand?"

Jamie tried the command again. And again, Barkley followed right behind him.

"Okay, return to your dogs now and give

them some praise," Mrs. Redding said.

Jamie just stood there. Barkley saw all the other dogs being petted and hugged, but Jamie didn't praise him. *What did I do wrong?* Barkley wondered.

The class practiced the *heel* command for a while, then returned to the new lesson. "Stay," said the chorus of kids.

Barkley ignored the rest of the class and stayed as close to Jamie's leg as he could.

"No!" pleaded Jamie. "Get back there."

"Be sure to work on your *stay* command at home this week," said Mrs. Redding. "Next week we'll walk away even farther from the dogs and make them wait longer before they can move. Before we finish tonight, though, I'd like you to try one more thing. When I say FAST, I want you to run. Make your dog work to keep up with you. Then when I say SLOW, just creep along."

Everyone looked around at each other, not really sure what they were supposed to do.

"Okay, FAST!" Mrs. Redding shouted.

Suddenly, the whole class began to race

around. Barkley loved it. "Ruff," he said, dancing sideways. "Ruff, ruff."

Then some of the other dogs joined in Barkley's dancing, too. They were all barking and prancing at the same time. Barkley happened to catch the German shepherd staring at him. He saw the determined look in the shepherd's eyes.

"Grrrr," the big dog growled as he leaped at Barkley.

The schnauzer panicked! He needed a place to hide—and FAST! The first place Barkley spotted was the refreshment table.

Two mothers were busy laying cookies and brownies in rows on fancy plates on top of the table. There was a huge bowl filled with bright purple punch and lots of shiny red cherries. And some gooey doughnuts sat right in the center of the table.

The women looked up just in time to see two dogs and two boys flying toward them. The cookies the women had been holding flew high into the air as the women took off in opposite directions. One of the doughnuts

landed smack on an Irish setter's head, and another stuck to the wall. The cookies and doughnuts were immediately attacked by 10 hungry dogs.

The punch landed everywhere, creating a goopy, gloppy, purple mess all over the floor. A peppy, white poodle now had a bright purple stripe down its back. And Sarge had a soaked head. He lay in the middle of all the craziness licking the purple punch off the floor.

Barkley escaped safely to the corner. He didn't try to grab any of the free food. *I'd rather be as far away from that disgusting shepherd as I can*, he decided. When Sarge wasn't looking, Barkley walked over to Jamie and licked his face.

Jamie was too upset to scold Barkley for ruining the after-class party. Jamie just wanted to go home and never come back. Barkley was hopeless. Things calmed down a little, and some of the kids started to leave.

"Hold it!" Mrs. Redding demanded. "Who started all of this?"

Devon jumped quickly to his feet and wiped

punch off his face with his sleeve. "That stupid dog of Jamie's started this mess," he shouted. "He's the one who did it, all right."

Jamie stood up, too. "No, this wasn't Barkley's fault," he said. "It was your dog who started it. He was chasing after Barkley."

"He was not!"

"He was, too!" Jamie said.

"Boys, now stop it," said Mrs. Redding. "What's done is done. Let's have everyone just sit down and calm down for a few minutes."

Devon and Jamie glared at each other as they took their seats.

"At least this class is never dull," said Mrs. Redding after a few deep breaths to calm her nerves. "Now, what did I want to tell you? Oh yes, there's a dog show that is being held during the county fair. Most dog shows require lots of training before you're able to enter," Mrs. Redding explained. "But this year the festival committee has added a category just for beginners."

"Yeah!" the kids shouted.

"How do we get in it?" Devon asked.

Mrs. Redding gave them all the details and handed out entry blanks. When Jamie reached for one, Devon shot him a nasty look.

"You're not going to enter, are you?" he sneered under his breath.

"Yes, I am," Jamie said. "Does that bother you?"

"That stupid dog of yours will mess up the whole show," Devon said.

"Not if your creepy dog stays out of his way," Jamie replied. "He's always chasing Barkley and scaring him. Just keep him away, and Barkley will be fine."

Devon saw Mrs. Redding watching them, so he turned and pulled Sarge in the other direction.

"Hey, did you hear the good news?" Melissa asked as she walked up behind Jamie. "They've added a section for beginners, so you and Barkley can enter the contest with Sadie and me."

"Yeah, I heard," Jamie said. "But I'm not so sure I can train Barkley in time for the contest."

"We'll do it. Don't worry," Melissa said. "That is, if I help you some more. We're a team now, right?"

"Right," Jamie said. He was excited to have a real friend in Indiana. He couldn't keep from grinning.

Ten

MELISSA came over to Jamie's house again the next night. She was eager to help her new friend teach Barkley how to behave in class.

They practiced all of the *heel* lessons. Barkley did great every time! They tried heeling forward, sideways, and in a figure eight. Barkley acted like he was already a 4-H class graduate!

Next, they worked on the *stay* command. But Barkley flunked every time. No matter what they tried to do, Barkley refused to listen. He stayed close to Jamie's leg wherever his master went.

Melissa tried holding Barkley while Jamie walked away. But whenever Barkley knew he was free to run, he scampered right over to

Jamie. They tried the command over and over again. Finally, on the ninth try, Barkley stayed still and waited for a few seconds.

Jamie and Melissa looked at each other and grinned. Melissa backed away a few steps, and Barkley started to get up. Quickly, Melissa stepped back toward the dog, and Barkley sat back down. Melissa moved away again, and Barkley started to get up again.

It became a game to Barkley. Every time Melissa moved very far from him, he stood up. And when Melissa moved back toward Barkley, the dog sat back down. He was doing just the opposite of what he was supposed to do.

"This isn't working," Melissa said at last. "We need something that will correct him the minute he tries to get up."

"Yeah," Jamie agreed. "But what?"

They sat down on the front porch to think. Barkley sat down, too.

After a while, Jamie said, "How about using a squirt gun?"

Melissa frowned, then smiled. "Yeah," she

84

said, "you know, it just might work. Do you have one around here?"

"I think I do. Come on," Jamie said. They were on their feet in an instant and running toward the house.

Jamie led the way into the house, up the stairs, and into his room. Barkley stayed close behind them. He was trying to figure out what the next game was going to be.

Jamie opened his closet door and began to toss things out on the floor, on his bed, and everywhere there was room.

"Ah. Here it is," said Jamie. He handed the bright green squirt gun to Melissa.

And away they went. They ran to the kitchen to load up the squirt gun and back out into the yard. Melissa picked her spot and waited. Jamie had Barkley sit down next to him.

"Now, stay," said Jamie, flashing the hand signal and walking off. Barkley was on his feet immediately, but he was in for a surprise.

Splat! A stream of water hit him right in the nose. He was so surprised by the cold water that he sat back down.

"Yahoo, it worked!" Jamie cheered, and he started jumping around the yard. Barkley was so happy to have done something right that he started prancing around the yard, too.

"Oh, Barkley," Melissa wailed. "You're supposed to stay still. You're not supposed to move around yet."

Melissa pulled out the squirt gun to let Barkley know that he did something wrong again, but the last drops of water just trickled out of the gun.

"Jamie, don't move around like that. How is Barkley going to learn what is right and wrong? Just stand still and look grouchy until the command is over."

"Sorry," said Jamie sheepishly. "Can we try it again?"

"Sure," said Melissa, "as soon as I reload the gun with water."

When she got back, they took their places again. Jamie repeated the order to stay.

Again, Barkley started to get up, and again he was squirted with water. Jamie could tell that Barklcy was beginning to make the connection. Even so, Barkley tried to get up once more.

Splat! He sat down and behaved from then on.

*   *   *   *   *

That night at dinner, Jamie told his parents about their new method for teaching Barkley to obey.

"I have even bigger news," Jamie said.

"What's that?" his dad asked.

"There's a dog show coming up. It's a contest where the dogs perform what they've learned in class. This is the first year they're letting beginners enter the show. I want to be in it," Jamie continued.

"Are you sure that's what you want?" his mother asked.

"What if Barkley won't cooperate in the contest?" his father asked.

"We'll be okay," Jamie said confidently. "Melissa and I have worked hard to train him."

"Okay, but just do your best. Don't expect

to go all out and win. That kind of contest is simply meant to be fun," Mrs. Boggs said.

"Okay, Mom," Jamie said. But he really did want to win the show.

"I'm really proud of you for sticking with it and teaching Barkley how to listen to you. He's not an easy dog to train," his mom grinned.

"Thanks, Mom," Jamie said. "It has really been kind of fun."

*   *   *   *   *

Before class began the next Monday, Mrs. Redding looked even more surprised about Jamie's decision than his parents had.

Jamie knew that he would have to prove Barkley was smarter than everyone in class thought he was. But for a minute, Jamie thought that Mrs. Redding might turn him and Barkley down.

"Jamie, you have to admit that Barkley has never behaved very well in class," she pointed out. "And unless something really big happens in the next class or two, I don't see how Barkley will listen during the show."

"Melissa has been helping me with him," Jamie said. "And he's doing better now."

Mrs. Redding just smiled politely. Jamie knew that she didn't believe him.

It seemed like Barkley had heard Mrs. Redding's doubts about his ability, too. For the first time, Barkley's performance sparkled. He did everything perfectly. And even when they tried the *stay* command for a longer time, Barkley waited patiently until Jamie gave the okay for him to move. The other kids watched in amazement.

"Wow! Barkley did really great tonight," said the girl with the collie.

"Yeah, a million times better than last week," another girl agreed.

"Gee, thanks," said Jamie. "I hope he does this well at the show next Saturday."

* * * * *

Melissa and Jamie worked with Barkley every night. Some nights, Melissa brought Sadie along, so she could get some practicing in, too. Melissa planned to enter Sadie in the advanced category.

Whenever Sadie came along, Barkley felt like showing off for her. When it was his turn to perform, he tried to do the best he could. Jamie squealed with delight every time Barkley did something right.

Each morning, Barkley still leapt through the hole in the garage wall and made his way to Mrs. Williams's house. He was thrilled that no one had caught on to his tricks yet. Having Mrs. Williams for a friend was the best!

One day, Mrs. Williams even fed Barkley a big, juicy hamburger. Then she brought out an old piece of carpeting and laid it on the porch for Barkley to take his nap on. Afterward, they had taken a short walk together through her garden. *What a great day it had been*, thought Barkley.

This morning, as usual, Barkley jumped through the wall and bounded down the road. He couldn't wait to find out what kind of treat Mrs. Williams would give him today. He loved the sound of her cheerful voice whenever he walked over to be petted.

But as Barkley rounded the last corner and saw her house up ahead, he didn't see her. She always waited on the porch for him to arrive. After he got there each day, they would have breakfast together. *Where was she?* Barkley wondered.

Her porch swing was empty, and he couldn't find her anywhere. He ran around to the garden to see if she was looking at all of her flowers. But she wasn't there. He looked around the yard, the field, and even through the front porch windows. But Barkley still couldn't find Mrs. Williams!

He knew something was wrong. But what? And what should he do? He had no idea where Jamie or Mr. and Mrs. Boggs were. And he didn't want to get lost like he had during their crazy move to Indiana. *That had been enough adventure for a lifetime,* Barkley thought.

"Ruff," Barkley said loudly, pawing at the door. But Mrs. Williams didn't come. He tried barking at the back door. There was still no answer.

Puzzled and scared, Barkley jumped up on his hind legs and peered through the kitchen window. *Yipes!* he thought. There was Mrs. Williams, laying flat on the floor. And she wasn't moving!

"Ruff! Ruff! Ruff!" Barkley said frantically. He had to get inside the house. He had to wake her up and make sure she was okay.

Barkley ran around and around the house, looking for an open window that he could leap through. But every one of them was either shut or too high for him to reach.

Barkley's head was spinning. He had to save Mrs. Williams. She was the best friend he'd ever had besides Jamie. He just had to get help for her!

He howled in frustration and ran out to the dusty road. It was completely deserted.

Where are those nice people who cleaned up her house and her garden? Barkley thought. *They would help me. But who are they and where do they live?*

Barkley looked up and down the road again, but there was still no sign of anyone. *Some-*

body please come, Barkley begged silently as he brushed some road dust off his nose with his paw. *Please come before it's too late.*

Then, suddenly, Barkley knew what he had to do. He took off across the field at full speed.

Eleven

BARKLEY forced his little legs to run faster through the tall, grassy field. When he finally reached the edge of the field, he looked both ways for the little jelly-fingered kids. *Nope, they're nowhere in sight,* Barkley thought gratefully.

Barkley ran across the lawn toward the house. He could see that mean broom woman through the window. She had the phone to her ear and was looking the other way.

He ran as close as he could to the window and called out to her. "Ruff, ruff," he said.

The broom woman turned around quickly. He was afraid of being hit again, but he kept telling himself that this was no time to be scared. The woman slammed the phone down on its hook. She picked up her broom and burst out the front door of the house.

"You dumb dog!" she shouted at him. "What are you doing back here again? I told you to stay away."

She clutched the broom tightly in her fingers. Barkley began barking to let her know that this was serious. He wasn't coming by just to play or to make her mad.

"Get out of here," the woman yelled as she swung her broom through the air.

Barkley kept right on barking and dodging her broom.

"I will not stand for this," she said. "You have no right to bother me. No right at all!" She took a step closer to Barkley and just missed hitting him with her broom.

Barkley ducked and ran away from her. As the woman swung at him again, Barkley grabbed onto the end of the broom with his teeth and held on with all his strength.

"That does it," the woman yelled angrily. "I've had enough of you. I'm calling the sheriff to come and take you away."

With that, Barkley tugged at the broom so

hard that a big chunk of it came off in his mouth. The woman's eyes flashed with anger. *This is my only chance,* he thought. *I have to make this work!*

Barkley took off running across her lawn and into the field. She chased after him, holding her broom. Barkley looked back at her every few seconds to make sure she was still following him. Once, when he thought she might give up, he ran around behind her and then back out in front. He knew she was mad enough now to keep up the chase.

As they neared Mrs. Williams's house, the broom woman started screaming.

"Myrtle, this dog is crazy! Call the sheriff! Call him now!"

Barkley hoped that her screams would help somehow. He ran up on the porch and barked as loud as he could. He had to show the broom lady where Mrs. Williams was.

Barkley looked up at her. She was leaning against the porch pillars trying to catch her breath. The schnauzer jumped off the porch and barked for her to follow him.

Instead, she glared at him and called out again. "Myrtle, are you there? Call the sheriff!"

The woman climbed the porch stairs and tried to open the front door. It was locked. Then she followed Barkley around to the back door, but it wouldn't open either.

Barkley stood in front of the kitchen window and barked as fast as he could. Finally, the woman caught on. She peered through the window and saw Mrs. Williams.

"Good heavens! Oh, Myrtle!"

The broom lady tried to use her weight to push the door open. The door creaked a little, but refused to give. Then, she found an old board that had been propped up against the house. She grabbed it and ran straight into the door. The rickety old door caved in.

Barkley quickly jumped over the door and led the way toward his friend. He licked her face and knew that she was alive. The broom lady put her ear up to the woman's mouth, then held onto her wrist for a few seconds. Barkley decided she must have been trying to figure out how sick Mrs. Williams was.

While the broom lady made a phone call, Barkley licked Mrs. Williams's hand to let her know that he was there by her side. *She would be all right now, wouldn't she?* Barkley wanted to know. *She just had to be okay.*

A few minutes later, Barkley heard a loud, strange noise outside. Then, he saw a flashing light as the broom lady ran to the front door. She opened it, and two men ran inside.

"I'm so glad you're here," the broom lady said to the ambulance attendants.

"Where is she?" one of the men asked.

"Back in the kitchen. It looks like she might have fallen. She's unconscious, and her leg looks like it may be hurt," the broom lady explained.

After a closer look, one of the attendants said, "I think you may be right. Her leg looks like it is pretty banged up."

The other man was busy using some medical instruments on Mrs. Williams. Suddenly, he looked up. "Who are you?" he asked the broom lady. "Are you a relative?"

"Oh, no. I'm just a neighbor," she explained. "I hardly ever come over here. But today this crazy dog came over to my house. He's bothered me before, but this time he wouldn't leave me alone. I finally started chasing him, and we ended up here at Mrs. Williams's house."

The man had a big smile on his face. "Wow! That's quite a story. I'd say this dog isn't crazy at all. In fact, he's a big-time hero," he pointed out. "This lady could have been here for a long time if he hadn't gotten you to follow him."

"You really think this dog led me here on purpose?" she said.

"Sure do," the same attendant said. "And it wouldn't be the first time that a dog was smart enough to do a brave thing like that."

Barkley eagerly watched all the activity going on around him. He couldn't keep his tail from wagging. He was so happy that Mrs. Williams had people to help her. He was sure that his friend would be all right now.

Barkley watched as they carefully lay Mrs. Williams on a long, cloth bed and wheeled her into the long object with the flashing light on top. It soon whirred to life and drove off down the dusty road.

Barkley wondered where they were taking his friend. He figured it was someplace that would make her better. He looked up at the broom lady and cautiously wagged his tail to thank her for helping Mrs. Williams.

To Barkley's surprise, she smiled back. "I was wrong about you," she said as she knelt down to give him a pat on the head. "And I'm really sorry. From now on, you're welcome to come over and play with Zach and Maria whenever you'd like to, okay?"

Barkley knew that whatever she was saying was nicer than before. And that was good enough for him.

"Ruff, ruff," he replied.

Twelve

THE day of the county fair dog show was bright and sunny. Jamie was up early that morning. He picked out his lucky outfit: his oldest T-shirt, his favorite shorts, and a baseball cap that his grandfather had given him a few years ago.

Barkley was all ready for the big show, too. He smelled fresh from the long bath Jamie had given him the night before. Jamie had even used a special brush to remove all the tangles in his fur.

But only one thing was bothering Barkley. He was worried about his friend, Mrs. Williams. Was she all right? He had no way of knowing if she was okay.

After breakfast, the Boggs family piled into the car and headed for the fair. The fair was so crowded that they had to park the car a long way from the fairgounds. There were tents and bicycles and people crowded together on the grass. The wonderful smells of cotton candy and caramel popcorn filled the air. There was even circus music playing.

Barkley wanted to take time to look around. There were babies crying and dogs scampering everywhere looking for food and fun.

But before Barkley could decide where to head first, he felt Jamie tugging at him impatiently. Barkley looked up at his master, whose eyes were fixed on a small roped-off area where a bunch of kids and dogs were gathering.

It was the show arena where Jamie and Barkley would be performing in just a little while. Looking around at the growing crowd made Jamie nervous. And he didn't feel any better when he spotted Devon and Sarge standing in the arena.

"I sure hope Barkley remembers everything I taught him in class," Jamie said to his parents.

In just a few minutes, it was time to begin! Jamie and Barkley headed for the arena. Suddenly, they were face to face with the German shepherd.

Barkley cringed as the boys glared at each other. "Why did you have to show up?" Devon sneered at them.

"Why did you?" Jamie shot back angrily.

"Because Sarge is going to win, that's why," Devon replied.

"Oh, yeah? Want to bet?" Jamie asked.

Mrs. Redding walked up behind them. "Okay, boys. That's enough," she interrupted. "Stop arguing right now, or I'll see that you're both disqualified from the contest."

The boys stopped fighting. But Barkley could tell by the look in their eyes that they were still mad at each other.

Just then, Barkley spotted Melissa and Sadie. He dragged Jamie toward them. Melissa was busy peering into her dog's throat.

"What are you doing? What's the matter?" Jamie asked worriedly.

"Oh, nothing," said Melissa. "I was just

checking Sadie's teeth. I wanted to see how clean they looked. Every detail is important, you know."

"So, are they clean?" Jamie asked worriedly. Barkley's teeth were one thing that he hadn't considered.

"Not bad, I guess," Melissa said. "My mom gave me an old toothbrush to use on Sadie's teeth. Sadie still has bad breath, but her teeth look a little whiter."

Jamie thought about checking out Barkley's teeth. He thought about asking his mom if she had a toothbrush for emergencies in her purse. He was sure that Barkley's teeth were yellow.

But, no, that was crazy! What dog worried about keeping his teeth shiny and white? Jamie wondered. This whole competition thing was getting out of hand.

* * * * *

After what seemed like hours, a man in a straw hat appeared with a microphone. "Ladies and gentlemen," he said. "May I have your attention? We're about to start the annual dog show now, so please gather around the arena."

The kids moved in closer.

"Our first contest is for beginning handlers," the announcer explained.

"That's you," said Melissa, giving Jamie a shove.

"When I call out your name," the man went on, "you will sit your dog at the entrance to the ring. At my signal you will *heel* to the first corner, then turn left, speed up for a short distance, and then finish by walking normally."

Barkley sat down on the ground and began to scratch frantically at his ear. Jamie looked down at him and frowned. He swatted at Barkley's paw to make him stop.

"Do a *halt* before turning the second corner. Then do a slow *heel*. Next, walk your dog normally, then walk around the third corner, and stop again just inside the entrance. We'll all do the *sit-stay* as a group at the end of the class. Okay, do any of you have a question before we begin the competition?"

The kids exchanged panicky looks, but no one said anything.

"All right, then," said the man. "Let's start with Jamie Boggs and Barkley."

Jamie gulped. He couldn't believe their bad luck. Why did they have to go first? For an instant, he had visions of Barkley laying down for a nap in the middle of the performance. He ran a nervous hand over Barkley's neck and looked around for his parents. They waved encouragingly.

"Are you ready, Jamie?" the announcer asked.

"Oh, sure," Jamie replied quickly. "Okay, come on, Barkley. Remember what we've practiced. Now is the time to show these people your stuff. Show them what you can do."

Barkley felt his master's light tug on the leash as he pulled him into the center of the arena. He sensed that Jamie was afraid. He felt that his master was worried about some kind of danger. Barkley decided that he'd better check out everything just to be sure.

As they passed the ropes that went around the arena, Barkley sniffed at them carefully. He decided that the judge and the announcer both looked kind of weird. He would definitely have to keep an eye on them.

"Sit," commanded Jamie. But Barkley knew that this was no time to be sitting down. He was watching for trouble.

"Sit," the boy repeated. When Barkley still ignored him, Jamie pushed down on the dog's behind.

Ouch! That hurt! Barkley thought. He gave Jamie an impatient glance.

Jamie looked up at the crowd to see if they were laughing at him and Barkley. But no one was—yet. "Please, Barkley, behave, okay?" Jamie pleaded.

But Barkley's eyes were glued to the announcer. He was convinced that the announcer was the cause for Jamie's fears.

"Barkley, heel," said Jamie as he began to walk forward. Suddenly, Barkley felt a tight pull at his neck as his master urged him to walk along beside him. Barkley fell forward and scrambled to catch up again.

This time, a few kids in the crowd began to giggle. Barkley turned to see what was so funny, and he tripped. The kids laughed even louder.

Jamie just wanted the whole thing to be over. He was so embarrassed. He could just imagine Devon and Sarge coming out for their performance. They would win for sure—and he'd never hear the end of it!

Jamie reached the first corner. Barkley was so busy staring down the announcer that he got left behind at the first corner. Even Barkley knew he goofed up that time.

Barkley decided he had better think about what he was doing. He took a deep breath and threw his shoulders back. He held his head up high and performed two turns perfectly. Before he knew it, the contest was over, and they were being led to the far end of the line.

The collie was next. He drew his share of hoots and hollers for doing things wrong. Most of the dogs seemed nervous and distracted by all the people. It certainly was different from

practicing in class.

Then it was Devon and Sarge's turn. Sarge performed everything just right, but he looked completely disgusted through the whole thing. He would sit when told to and come when requested. But then he gave the audience a silly look like he was bored and couldn't wait to get out of there.

After all of the dogs had finished the individual competition, the announcer asked everyone to take their places for the group competition.

"Line up around the outside rope," the announcer called out. "Space your dogs at least three feet apart. We don't want any dog to be distracted because it likes the dog next to him or her."

Everyone laughed. The announcer waited until all of the dogs were in place.

"Okay, everyone, if your dog disqualifies itself by moving before it is signaled to do so, then walk outside of the ring with your dog. Okay, now, gang, leave your dogs," he said. "Start walking away from them very slowly."

"Stay," said the chorus of kids, waving their hands in front of the dogs' faces as they had learned in class. The kids walked to the far side of the ring and turned around.

A cute mutt thought it was supposed to heel and was instantly out of the event. Next, the collie grew bored and walked off. A couple other dogs followed their lead.

Barkley remembered the squirt gun. He knew what he was supposed to do this time. He knew this command well and was determined to make Jamie proud of him. He settled in for a long wait. He yawned and let his eyes wander out over the crowd.

He noticed the ice cream cones. Boy, they looked good. He saw a cute little kitten snuggling in a girl's arms. He saw a little boy crying. He wished he could go play with him.

Suddenly, something caught Barkley's eye. He knew he was supposed to sit until Jamie told him it was okay to move. But he couldn't do it. He had to go.

In a single leap, Barkley bounded off the stage and away from his master.

Thirteen

"**B**ARKLEY, no! Don't do this. Come back here!" Jamie shouted as he watched his dog scamper away. But Barkley was too excited to go back to that silly test where he had to sit like a statue. Forget it!

The crowd watched eagerly as Barkley made his way into the crowd. Little kids reached out to pet him, but the schnauzer kept on running. There was no time to waste.

Barkley finally reached the edge of the crowd and stopped for a second. He looked ahead to where a few people sat quietly together. They were talking in soft voices and didn't notice him as he sat down beside them.

"Ruff, ruff," he said in a soft voice, so he wouldn't scare them.

Two men turned and looked at Barkley.

Then the last person of the group—the most important person—looked down at him from her wheelchair. For a second, she didn't seem to know him either. Barkley raised one paw and said, "Ruff."

The woman's eyes suddenly brightened, and she smiled.

"Oh, my goodness," she gasped. "I can't believe it's you!"

She held her arms open wide. Barkley jumped right up on her lap and licked her face. He was so happy! Mrs. Williams, his wonderful friend, was all right!

"It's my little Love. Where did you come from?" she asked.

Barkley's tail wagged like crazy. He wanted her to know how happy he was that she was okay now.

"Mom, what are you doing?" the man behind Mrs. Williams's chair asked. "Is that dog bothering you?"

"Never!" she replied with a big smile. "This dog could never bother me. He's the one I was telling you about, Tim," she said. "The one who

went to get me help the day I fell."

"That's him?" Tim asked. "Are you sure it's the same one?"

"Yes, I'm sure," Mrs. Williams said as she scratched Barkley behind the ears. "He always raises his paw like that."

"Well, then, I think he deserves a royal treat of some kind," Tim said.

Just then, Jamie came running up to them. When he saw that Barkley had made himself comfortable in Mrs. Williams's lap, his eyes grew wide.

"Gosh, I'm so sorry, ma'am," he said. "Barkley doesn't usually get so carried away. I mean, he's friendly, and he likes people and all. But he doesn't usually jump right up on people's laps. Come here, Barkley."

Barkley didn't move. He hadn't had a long enough visit with Mrs. Williams.

"His name is Barkley?" she asked. "Is he your dog?"

"Yes, he is," Jamie admitted. "We were up there in the show arena and Barkley just took off. I was trying to make him sit, but he had other ideas. I'm really surprised he just jumped up on you like that. I'm so sorry. He doesn't usually act this way."

"But why would you be sorry to have a wonderful animal like this?" she asked him.

Jamie looked at her strangely. "Well, usually I'm not," he said. "But he just got himself disqualified from the dog show. We practiced the lessons a lot, and I was hoping that we'd do well today. But we didn't."

The woman stroked Barkley's neck thoughtfully. "Yes, I can understand your disappointment, especially with him running off the platform like that," Mrs. Williams said. "But your dog and I are good friends. And he was worried about me."

Jamie looked puzzled. "What do you mean? I don't understand."

"Your dog visits with me every day," she explained. "We have a great time. We have lunch together and walk around the garden when it's nice outside. Sometimes we even fall asleep and take naps on my porch."

"No," Jamie said. " It can't be Barkley. He's

locked in the garage every day while my parents work and I'm at school," he said.

"Yes, that's right," Mr. Boggs said as he and Mrs. Boggs walked up behind Jamie. "He's always there in the afternoon when Mom comes home, isn't he, Jamie?"

"Yeah. Barkley sleeps in a little bed of old rags that he's collected. Whenever I open the garage door, he runs out to meet me," Jamie explained. "He's never gotten out."

The beginner's half of the dog show had ended, and a few of the kids came over to see where Barkley had gone.

Mrs. Williams introduced herself and then smiled. "Well, let me try a little test to see if he is the same schnauzer who visits me," she said. "Okay?"

Jamie and his father nodded.

Mrs. Williams set Barkley on the ground and reached inside her purse. She pulled out a cookie. It was a peanut butter cookie, Barkley's favorite.

"It's cookie time!" she announced joyfully.

Barkley wagged his tail. He quickly raised

one paw and said, "Ruff."

Mrs. Williams grinned. "See?" she asked. "That's a little game we play. I assume you taught that to him, young man."

"Yes, yes I did," Jamie mumbled in disbelief. "But I don't understand how he..."

Mrs. Williams smiled. "Oh, your dog and I have shared a lot together," she said. "In fact, you could even say that he saved my life."

Mr. Boggs moved in closer. "What do you mean, Mrs. Williams?" he asked.

"Well, last week, I had a bad fall in my kitchen," she began. "I ended up cracking a bone in my leg, as you can see by this cast. I also got quite a bump on the head when I fell."

She hesitated, then continued. "I was unconscious for quite a while. But Barkley here somehow discovered that I needed help and ran to the neighbor's. He barked and barked until she followed him. Then he led her to me."

"Barkley did all that?" Jamie asked in amazement. Barkley was pretty terrific all right, but was he smart enough to track someone down to get help? Was this the same Barkley who refused to heel and stay? It was hard to believe.

"He sure did," Tim spoke up. "Mom talks about him all the time. It's hard for me or my brother, Darrel, to check on Mom as often as we'd like to. If she had a dog like Barkley around to keep an eye on her, it would mean a lot to us, and to her. What I'm trying to say is that we'd like to buy Barkley for Mom. He really means a lot to her."

"Yes, just name your price, and we'll be glad to pay it," Darrel said. "Barkley has done so much for us already."

"Uh, no, Barkley's my dog," Jamie said. "There's no way I'd sell him. He means a lot to me, too." Jamie added. "Barkley's not for sale."

"Yes, that's right," Mr. Boggs agreed. "Barkley's an important member of our family. But maybe we could work out an arrangement. Mrs. Williams, how would you like to be our official daytime baby-sitter for Barkley? And when we go on vacations or away for the weekend, we'd love it if you'd take care of

Barkley for us. We'll supply all of his food, of course."

"Well, I'll supply all of the cookies," Mrs. Williams said with a big smile.

"Hey," said Jamie with a smile. "I like cookies, too. Maybe I could come visit sometimes after I get home from school. I could even help you with some work around the house, like cutting grass and stuff like that."

Tim laughed. "Well, there sure is plenty of work to do. We would pay you. We're so busy with our farm that sometimes we don't get to work at Mom's place as often as we want to."

"All right, then. It's a deal," Mr. Boggs said.

"Yes," said his wife. "But I'm still puzzled about how Barkley managed to get out of the garage. It's a mystery that's driving me crazy."

"I'm sure you'll find the secret," Mrs. Williams said as she looked down at Barkley. "Hey, Barkley, do you understand the news? We're going to be together almost every day. Isn't that great?"

"Ruff, ruff," Barkley said.

They agreed that Mr. Boggs would drop off

Barkley at Mrs. Williams's house each morning on his way to work. Then after school, Jamie would go pick him up.

The Boggs family and Barkley said goodbye to Mrs. Williams and her sons. Then they walked closer to the platform to catch the end of the dog show. They got there just as Melissa was being handed a trophy.

"All right! Jamie cheered loudly. "Way to go!"

"What are you cheering about?" Devon asked loudly. "That mutt of yours didn't win anything. In fact, he didn't even stick around until the end of the competition."

Jamie turned around to give Devon a nasty look. Then he saw that Devon was waving a bright red ribbon proudly in the air. Sarge was laying in the grass behind him. For once, the shepherd looked more bored than mean.

Jamie thought about being a nice guy and congratulating Devon for his win. But the other kids began talking before he could say anything.

"Boy, you sure don't know much, Devon.

Barkley's a real-live hero!" said one of the girls who had heard the whole story.

"Yeah," agreed the little girl with the collie. "Barkley got help for a lady who fell. He saved her life! And that's much more important than any old ribbon."

"No way!" Devon said. "Barkley's too stupid to do anything like that. You're just making it up, because you're all jealous of Sarge and me."

Then Devon noticed that Mr. Boggs was standing next to Jamie. "It's great that you won that ribbon," Jamie's dad said to Devon. "It means you did a good job of training your dog. But, no, these kids aren't making up anything. Barkley did do something pretty terrific. He got help for Mrs. Williams when she fell."

"I think Barkley should have a ribbon, too," said Danielle.

Jamie shook his head. "It's okay. We don't need a ribbon. I'm just proud of Barkley for being a great dog," he said as he patted his schnauzer on the head.

Just then, a woman and a man with a camera on his shoulder interrupted them.

"Excuse me," said the woman. "We're from Channel 10 Action News and we'd like to get a short story about the dog who saved Mrs. Williams for tonight's news program. Can you lead us to where Mrs. Williams is sitting? Bring your dog along so that we can film all three of you together."

Jamie and Mr. Boggs led the way to where Mrs. Williams was seated. Barkley sat down next to her wheelchair, and Jamie stood beside her, too.

The cameraman pointed his camera at them. A little light came on and the woman reporter started talking about Barkley. She asked Jamie and Mrs. Williams some questions.

Barkley waited for a while, but then he started to feel hungry again. Mrs Williams had only given him one cookie, and it was getting close to lunchtime. He looked up at the woman with the microphone. She looked nice. Maybe she had a cookie for him.

"Ruff!" Barkley said, lifting up his paw.

The man with the camera aimed it at the little schnauzer and everyone laughed.

"How about three cheers for Barkley?" Melissa suggested.

"Hip hip hurray, hip hip hurray, hip hip hurray!" all the kids yelled.

Barkley danced around for the camera as Jamie and Mrs. Williams filled the reporter in on what had happened.

They said good-bye to Mrs. Williams and her sons again and walked the long way back to their car.

"Wow, what a day this has been," Mrs. Boggs said during the drive home. "I still can't get over what Barkley did." She turned around and patted the schnauzer on the head.

As soon as they pulled into the driveway, Jamie jumped out of the car. He lifted up the garage door and started poking around inside. It didn't take him long to solve the mystery.

"Hey, Mom, Dad," Jamie said. "Come look at this."

He pointed to the hole in the wall.

"Hey, I plugged that up not too long ago," Mr. Boggs said. "I used a bunch of old rags."

Jamie grinned. "So, that's how Barkley made his bed in the corner. It all makes sense now!"

Mrs. Boggs laughed. "Come on, let's go inside and have an early dinner. We don't want to miss our hero on TV tonight. Right, Barkley?"

"Ruff, ruff!" he said cheerfully.

About the Author

MARILYN D. ANDERSON grew up on a dairy farm in Minnesota. Her love for animals and her twenty-plus years of training and showing horses are reflected in many of her books.

A former music teacher, Marilyn has taught band and choir for seventeen years. She specializes in percussion and violin. She stays busy training young horses, riding in dressage shows, working at a library, giving piano lessons, and, of course, writing books. Marilyn and her husband live in Bedford, Indiana.

Nobody Wants Barkley is a sequel to *Barkley Come Home.*